To The Farm

Let's Go To The Farm

ABC Adventures

Written by Pat Whitehead

Illustrated by Ethel Gold

Troll Associates

Library of Congress Cataloging in Publication Data

Whitehead, Patricia.
 Let's go to the farm.

 (ABC adventures)
 Summary: Two children visit a farm and see all the
different animals. A letter of the alphabet appears on
each page accompanied by an appropriate word from the
text.
 1. Children's stories, American. [1. Farm life—
Fiction. 2. Domestic animals—Fiction. 3. Alphabet]
I. Gold, Ethel, ill. II. Title. III. Series: Whitehead,
Patricia. ABC adventures.
PZ7.W5852Le 1985 [E] 84-8834
ISBN 0-8167-0377-9 (lib. bdg.)
ISBN 0-8167-0378-7 (pbk.)

Come on. Let's go to the farm.

Aa

animals

There are animals on the farm.

Bb

baby

Here are some baby animals.

Cc

cow

This is a baby cow.

Dd

duck

This is a baby duck.

Ee

eat

This little duck likes to eat.

Ff

from

She eats from morning till night.

Gg

good

She looks for good things to eat.

Hh

horse

Here is a baby horse.

Ii

ivy

The baby horse is smelling ivy.

Jj

jumps

The baby pig jumps up when the farmer brings food.

Kk

kinds

The baby duck likes all kinds of food.

Ll

Listen

Listen! Listen to the baby animals.

Mm

moos

The baby cow moos.

Nn

neighs

The baby horse neighs.
"Neigh!"

Oo

oinks

The baby pig oinks.
"Oink, oink."

Pp

Peep

Even the baby chicks join in.
''Peep, peep!'' cry the little chicks.

Qq

quack

But what about the baby duck?
Why doesn't she quack?

Rr

rubs

She rubs her little tummy.
"Ooooh," she says.

Ss

sick

"I feel sick."

Tt

tummy

"My tummy hurts."

Uu

Ugh

"Ugh," she says.
"I guess I ate too much."

Vv

very

"I don't feel very well."
"Look. Here comes the animal doctor."

Ww

waddles

"Come to me," calls the doctor.
The baby duck waddles over.

Xx

examine

"Let me examine you," he says. "You will be fine."

Yy

yummy

Oh my, what's this?

"That looks yummy," quacks the little duck.
"I feel better already."

Zz

zips

The little duck zips over for her dinner.

"Quack, quack. Quack, quack."
Listen. Even the baby duck is singing now!